Dear Teacher

By Amy Husband

For James

Text and illustrations © 2010
by Amy Husband.
Cover and internal design © 2010 by
Sourcebooks, Inc.
Sourcebooks and the colophon are registered
trademarks of Sourcebooks, Inc.
All rights reserved.
Published by Sourcebooks Jabberwocky, an imprint
of Sourcebooks, Inc., Naperville, IL.
First published in Great Britain in 2009 by
Meadowside Children's Books.
CIP data is on file with the publisher.
Source of Production: Leo Paper, Heshan City, China
Date of Production: July 2010
Run Number: 12513
Printed and bound in China.
LEO 10 9 8 7 6 5 4 3 2 1

sourcebooks
jabberwocky

Sunnybank Elementary School

Friday, August 15th

Dear Michael,

We are looking forward to welcoming you back to school for the start of the new year. I hope you have had a really fun break and are ready to dive into lots of learning!

This year your class will be working especially hard in math, history, geography, and English. I am sure that if you study carefully, you will find those spelling tests can be a fun challenge!

Your new teacher is called Miss Brooks. She has all sorts of exciting plans for the new year. We look forward to seeing you on Monday.

Yours sincerely,

N.T Grindstone

Shhhh

TOP SECRET

the secret service man

Dear Teacher,

I might be a bit late for the first day of school. The weirdest thing happened today. The head of the **secret service** turned up!

They need me for a special **secret** mission to find a missing explorer. I did mention the math test, but he just said that the future of the country depends on me. I couldn't say no. <u>Sorry</u> Miss Brooks.

(Fingers crossed I'll be back in time for the test!)

From **Michael**

My dog Bruno

P.S. Bruno's coming with me— he makes a great bloodhound.

P.P.S. The stuff I've told you is **Top Secret**, so please eat this letter.

TOP SECRET

Missing Explorer

Dear Teacher,

The explorer was stuck on top of **Mount Everest!** We rescued him and Bruno was awesome! I've never seen a dog go that fast before. The explorer told me about an ancient treasure map hidden in **Egypt.** He has a bad cold, so he wants me to search for the map. (I did tell him I had to get back for the math test, but this is **really important.**)

I will probably only be a few hours late for the first day of school.

From **Michael**

P.S. Please don't let Nicholas sit in my place.

Honest, Miss Brooks, I didn't know it was going to the Amazon River! The map says the treasure is hidden there so I might as well find it.

From Michael

P.S. I'll really miss the homework.

✉ TELEGRAM

TEACHER.

AMAZON VERY HOT AND DANGEROUS.

NO SIGN OF TREASURE.

SORRY ABOUT RIPPED PAPER.   ATTACKED BY CROC.

LIVING OFF BEETLES AND SPIDERS.

REALLY MISS PEANUT BUTTER SANDWICHES.

WILL BE EVEN LATER NOW.

HIPPO ATE COMPASS.

MICHAEL.

P.S. OH NO! SNAKES CAN SWIM!

Post Card

The school trip to the zoo is **awesome!** In fact it's so good, I'm not coming home. The zookeeper asked me to stay here to work with the wild animals. Miss Brooks said it would be okay with you. Don't bother her about this though. I'll let you know when you can come for a visit. (Please send Bruno with some peanut butter sandwiches.)

From Michael x

P.S. Nicholas is working here too. I'm letting him do all the sweeping in the elephant and monkey habitats.

Dear
Mom
and
Dad

Miss C. Brooks

P.S. I saw your mother in the supermarket again today. Your baby brother was dressed as a pirate! What a coincidence! I nearly made a citizen's arrest as I thought he was the Pirate King.

Friday, August 29th

Sunnybank Elementary School

Dear Michael,

Thank you for your letters. It sounds as though you have been very busy.

I am sorry to hear you won't be coming back to school this year, there is so much planned that you would have enjoyed (not including all the tests). We are going to be playing lots of soccer this year; I expect Nicholas will have to be captain now, and there's the science fair at midterm where everyone gets to invent something.

We're going on a school trip to the zoo next week, you'd have loved it! You could have told everyone about hippos, snakes, dolphins, and, of course, crocodile wrestling (I'm not so sure about eating spiders though). We're also having swimming lessons, which I think you'd have been very good at. Bruno sounds like a very unusual dog. It would have been great to meet him on Pet's Day later this semester.

Take care on the moon, Michael, I hear it can get a bit boring up there. We will think of you when we're making our giant model of the solar system. We'll save your place for Monday morning in case you can make it to school after all.

C Brooks.

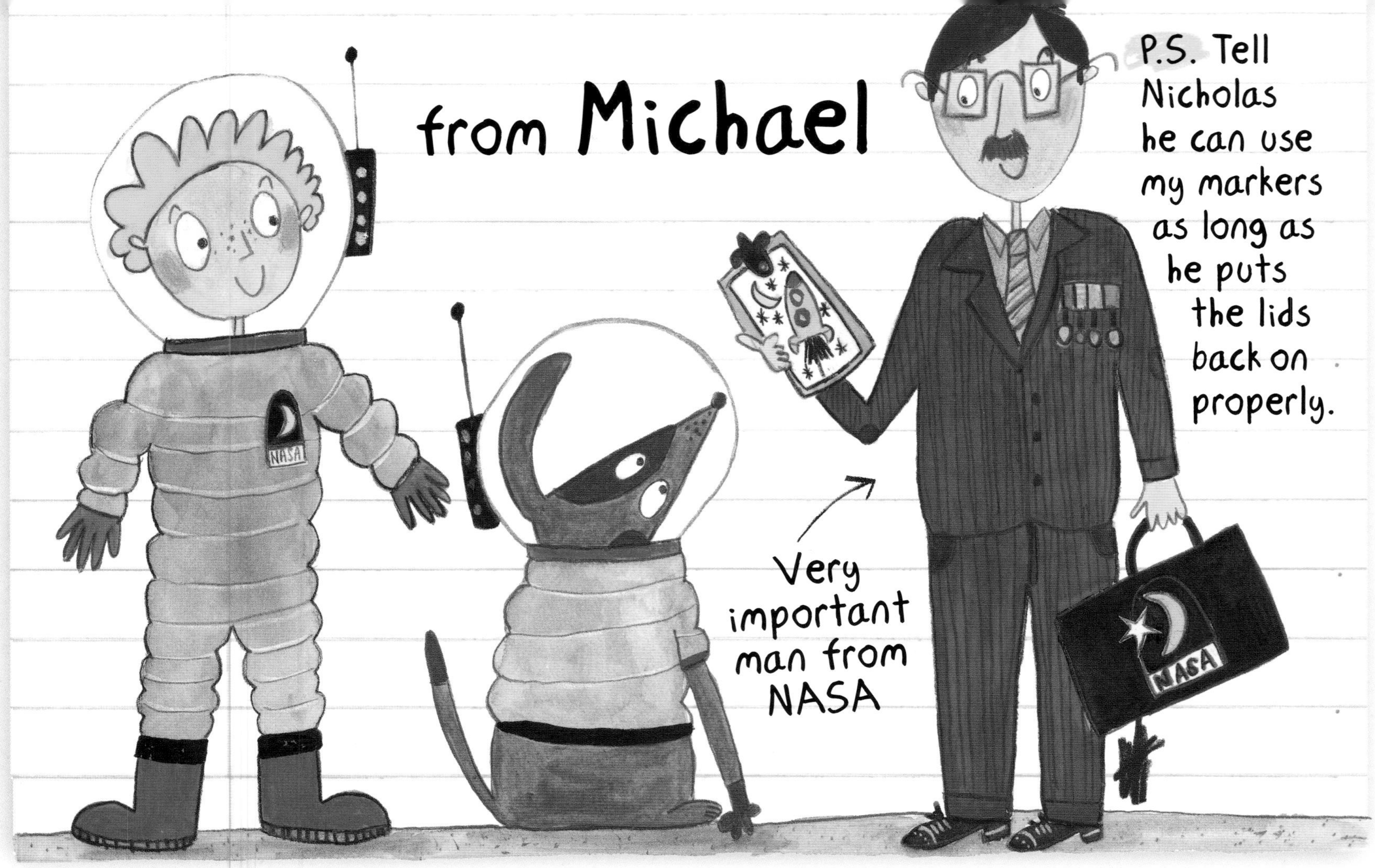
from Michael
P.S. Tell Nicholas he can use my markers as long as he puts the lids back on properly.
Very important man from NASA
NASA
NASA

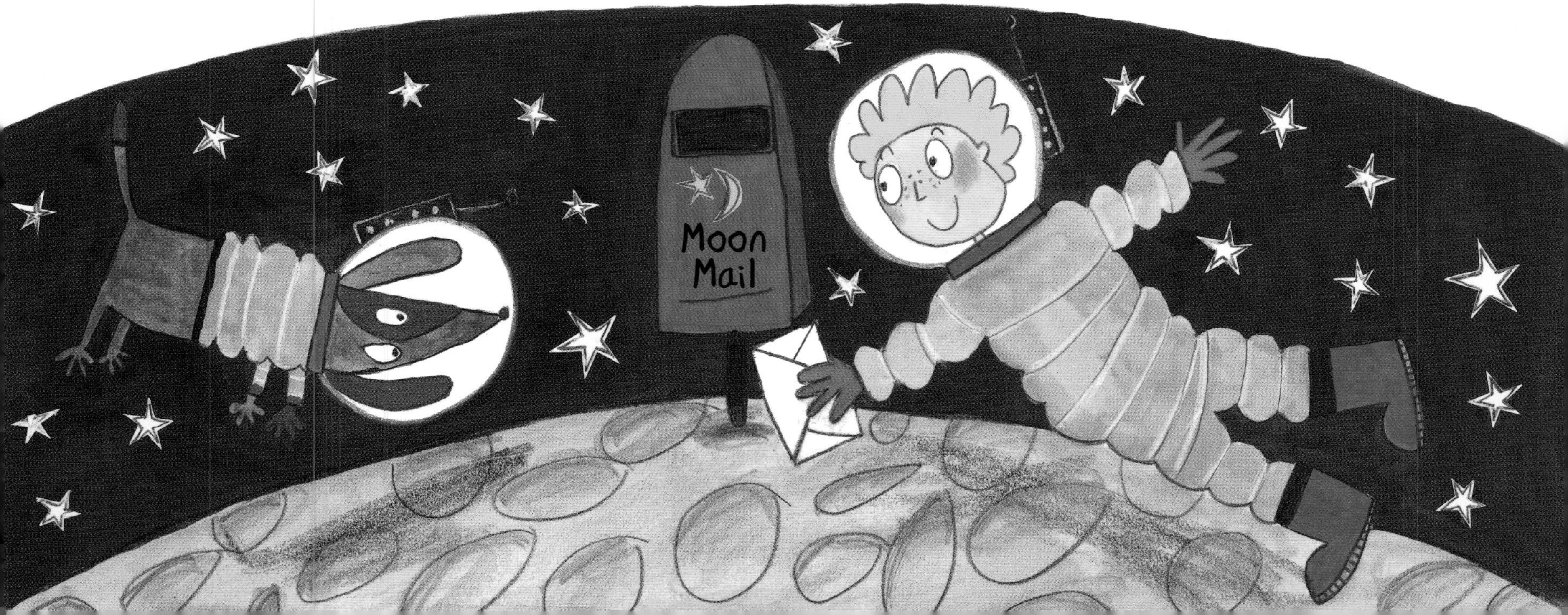
Moon Mail

Dear Teacher,

I've got some good news and some bad news. We caught the Pirate King trying to steal a rocket! Bruno and I stopped him though. Now for the bad news. I'm not going to be coming back ever. I'm really disappointed (especially about the science test.)

NASA wants me to go on a space mission. I'll be on the moon for a gazillion years. I told them about the math tests, but they said that the future of the planet has to come first. Bruno's coming too, so I won't be lonely.

From Michael

P.S. It's probably best not to mention this to Mom if you see her in the supermarket again.

Orient Express
Platform 3

Express Mail

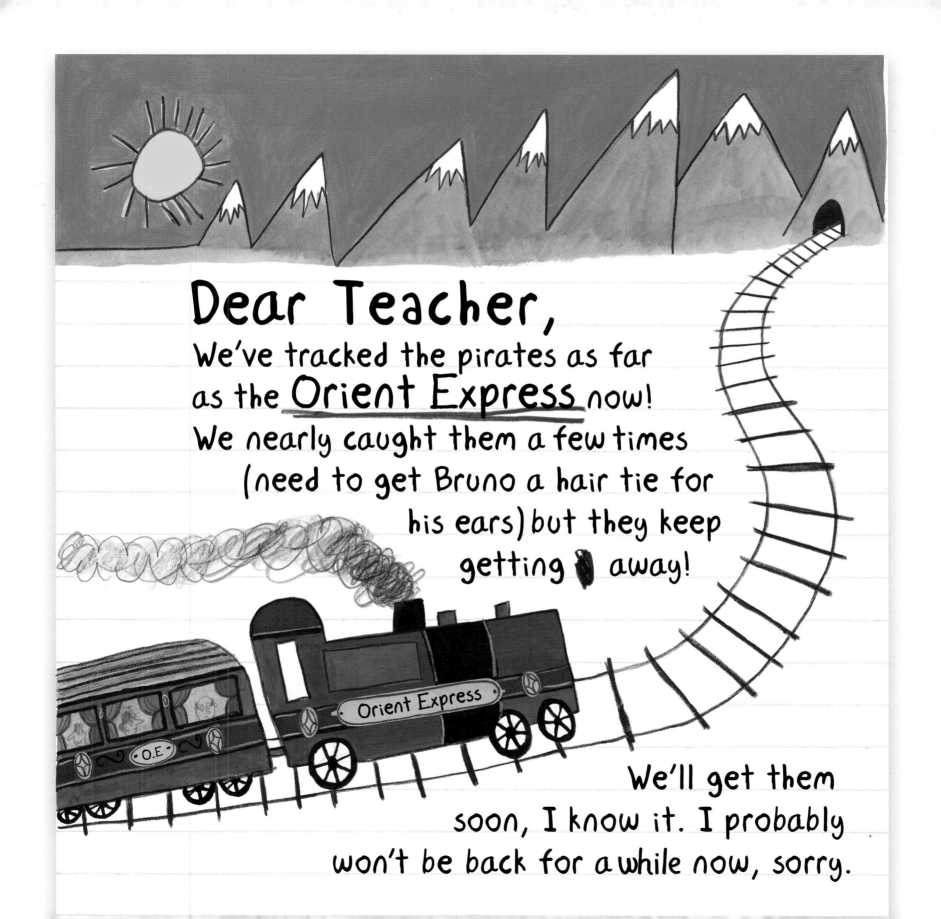

Dear Teacher,
We found out where the pirates are going, and we've hired an airplane to try to cut them off. Wish us luck! We'll be a little longer than I thought, but don't worry, Miss Brooks, ~~I~~ I can't wait to catch up on all the work.

From Michael

P.S. Bruno makes a super copilot, except when he tries to chase birds . . .

Dear Teacher,

We found a boat home but Pirates <u>attacked</u> us! The Pirate King tied us up, stole the treasure, and made us <u>walk the plank!</u> Thank goodness Bruno and I are such good swimmers. I'm going to get the treasure back. This could make me really, really late! I'm really sorry, Miss Brooks, but I can't let the Pirate King get away with this.

From Michael

P.S. Please don't let Nicholas use my markers.

P.P.S. I don't mind if he takes my turn at tidying the storage cupboard.

It was hidden behind a waterfall, not by a river! Bruno was holding the map the wrong way. (Never trust a dog with a map.)

We'll head home as soon as we can find some transportation. The bad news is, I'll be really late for the start of school, sorry.

From **Michael**

 P.S. This is all still  TOP SECRET so don't tell anyone.